The *Beauty* of a WOMAN

The *Beauty* of a WOMAN

Viktor G. Zubin

The Beauty of a Woman

Copyright © 2024 by Viktor G. Zubin. All rights reserved.

No part of this publication may be reproduced, stored in a retrieval system or transmitted in any way by any means, electronic, mechanical, photocopy, recording or otherwise without the prior permission of the author except as provided by USA copyright law.

The opinions expressed by the author are not necessarily those of URLink Print and Media.

1603 Capitol Ave., Suite 310 Cheyenne, Wyoming USA 82001
1-888-980-6523 | admin@urlinkpublishing.com

URLink Print and Media is committed to excellence in the publishing industry.

Book design copyright © 2024 by URLink Print and Media. All rights reserved.

Published in the United States of America
ISBN 978-1-68486-681-6 (Paperback)
ISBN 978-1-68486-684-7 (Digital)

23.01.24

Inspired by: a Russian song of the same name sung by Lx24.

PROLOGUE

There's a saying that goes something like this, "appreciate what you have before it disappears". I can say with 100% certainty that it's true. I bet you have no idea what I am talking about do you? Allow me to start at the very beginning, back when I was young, strong and thought that I have all the time in the world.

CHAPTER 1

I AM NOT READY!

On a hill, not far away from their village, a young couple were intengled in each other's arms. It is clear as day, that these young people were deeply infatuated with each other. Having just finished their picnic date, they were enjoying each other's company. The woman was very beautiful. She had golden hair as bright as the sun capable of attracting any man. She had an hour-glass figure and dark blue eyes. The man felt extremely lucky to be dating the most beautiful girl in the village.

The man wasn't bad looking either, but he wasn't stunningly handsome. He had black hair and was decently built. His only flaw, if you could call it that, was that He was laid back, and enjoyed his freedom.

The girl turned her head up and spoke to the man, "Alex, when are we gonna get married?"

Alex looked down on his girlfriend with an annoyed expression and said with a sigh, "Lilly, we have been through this many times already. We'll get married soon. Besides, what's the rush? We're young, we still got time"

Lilly sat up and got out of Alex's embrace and folded her arms clearly dissatisfied. " I don't know about you, but I want to have children while I am young and, God willing, I want to see my grandkids"

Clearly irritated, Alex got up and yelled, "CHILDREN! CHILDREN! CHILDREN! That is all you care about! What about freedom? Traveling the world? All we've ever known is this shit-hole where there is nothing. Endless early rises with the sun, gardening and taking care of the flock. If that wasn't enough, children are annoying. They cry, bellyache for every little thing. I am sorry, but I don't want to tie myself down with children yet. I AM NOT READY!"

CHAPTER 2

IT'S OVER!

Lily couldn't fathom what she was hearing. *Was this the same Alex I fell head-over-heels for?*

"IT'S OVER!" That is all Lily was able to blurt out. All the while she felt the world around her turn upside down. Her heart was beating so hard, she could barely contain it. However, instead of apologizing, Alex only escalated the situation.

"It's over?" He smiled sinisterly "Good, I don't have to worry about you any more. I was planning on leaving this place sooner or later, and you just helped me decide." Without a hint of remorse, Alex started his way down the hill to go and pack his things. *Big city here I come!* He thought to himself. Meanwhile, Lily stayed on that hill sobbing uncontrollably. What started out as a lovely picnic turned out to be the worst break-up in history. Lily cried for a long time on that hill. Eventually, she stopped crying and started putting away the picnic basket. Only one thought occupied her at that moment, *What am I to do now?*

CHAPTER 3

ALEX– THE HOMEWRECKER!

Alex was first to arrive at the village. Without speaking toanyone, he entered his home and started packing his things. Alex's mother heard the commotion and went to what the ruckus was all about. She was shocked to see that her son was packing his things. "Where are you going?" She inquired.

"I am leaving." Alex answered with a look of determination in his eyes, but not saying anymore.

"What is this all of a sudden? Did you and Lily have a fight?". The mother continued questioning, while at the same time, trying to stop her son from leaving. Alex knew that his mother would not stop questioning him until he answered her questions. Alex stopped packing, sighed deeply and said, "Lily and I…broke up". Hearing this, Alex's mother looked at her son with an angry expression and asked sternly with her hands on her hips, "What did you do?"

Alex felt sweat drops forming at the top of his forehead. Raising his arms in protest he answered saying, "I didn't do anything! All I did was tell Lily that I didn't want to get married and that we had plenty of time". Thinking that his explanation was sufficient, Alex thought that he was off the hook when his mother yelled at him.

"YOU SAID WHAT! ARE YOU CRAZY? I never thought that my son would grow up to be such a selfish man." At this point the mother could barely hold back tears. "Do you even care about your father and I? We are not as young as we used to be. Our dearest wish was to see our grandkids before we die. Now, because you have severed the relationship between you and Lily, that wish will never be granted" The mother sighed, disappointment clearly visible on her face. Before the mother left she said, "Pray that your father doesn't hear a word of this"

In his defense Alex said, "I was not the one that terminated the relationship, she did." Referring to Lily.

In response the mother said, "The truth will be revealed once Lily returns" With that, the mother left the room.

When Lily arrived at the village, a group of people were gathered together. It seems they were waiting for someone. Doing her best to wipe the tears off her face, Lily asked the crowd, "What's going on?". Instead of getting a reply, a muscular man with black hair with streaks of silver came up to her and slapped her on the cheek. "YOU LITTLE BRAT! How dare you break off your engagement to Alex? Don't you realize that your deed has brought shame to our family!"

At this point Lily started sobbing again, harder than she was previously. After she calmed down she started to explain saying, "I had no choice but to break it off. Alex called this place a shit-hole.

But, that is nothing compared to what he said next. Alex said that children are annoying and that he valued his freedom more than having a family and children."

Hearing this, the crowd's attitude changed drastically. Alex was called out of the house and questioned if everything that Lily had told them was true. Instead of being ashamed of his words and actions, Alex stood proudly admitting that what Lily said was true. He continued by saying that he was tired of the early rising to tend to the fields and much more.

The same muscular man that slapped Lily couldn't hold it anymore. He came to the front of the crowd and slapped Alex harder than he did Lily. "YOU ARROGANT PIECE OF SHIT! You would rather have your so-called 'freedom' instead of being a husband to my daughter. Lily did the right thing by dumping you. I will find a more suitable husband for Lily.``. The man turned around preparing to leave. "If you EVER come near my daughter again, I will kill you. Moreover, I will tell your father what you did and ask him to exile you from the village."

When Alex's father was informed of what had transpired, he was so angry that it was hard to recognize him. *My son is a true disappointment* the man thought to himself.

Having the crowd's attention, Alex's father declared, "Alex, for playing with Lily's feelings and bringing shame through your actions, you are hereby banished from the village! You are forbidden to return to this village ever again! However, because you are my flesh and blood I will give you some money. Use it however you see fit, and if you die, then you die"

This whole time Alex was speechless and didn't know what to say. All he managed to do was bow to his father for the last time, take the money and the bag that he had packed, all this was done without a single word. As Alex turned to leave, Lily called out to him yelling at him, "ALEX YOU HEARTLESS, HOMEWRECKER!"

Alex ignored Lily's screams without turning back. However, Alex had no idea what would happen to this village after he left

CHAPTER 4

WELCOME TO THE CITY

Alex arrived at the city using the money his dad gave him. Looking at the small amount of money left, enough for a few days at most, he sighed deeply and thought to himself, *I need a job ASAP.* Having decided on his next plan of action, Alex tried to get a job at many places. However, he was rejected at all of them. Either he wasn't experienced enough in the field, or his education level isn't high enough. The City Bank was his last choice, if Alex didn't get accepted here, he didn't know what he would do.

Taking a deep breath, Alex strode into the building through the front door. Alex went up to the receptionist at the front desk. "Hello, my name is Alex. I am looking for a job. Do you have any open vacancies?"

The receptionist replied "You are in luck, handsome, we have an opening as a security guard. Will you take it?"

"YES OF COURSE!" Alex yelled in excitement

"Shhhh", the receptionist made a hand gesture to her mouth signaling for Alex to quiet down. "If you want to take the security guard position, talk to the manager, he will tell you what to do" "Thank you very much". With that, Alex went off to the races to start his new job as a security guard at the City Central Bank.

CHAPTER 5

FACING THE PAST

10 Years Later

It's been 10 years huh? Time sure flies by fast. I haven't seen my parents in a long time, I should visit them to see how they're doing.

Sitting in his chair, in his office, Alex was reminiscing about the past ten years and what a journey it was to get to his current position. First he worked as a security guard for a while[after talking to the manager, who turned out to be a decent person].

Needless to say, Alex and the manager got very close. It didn't affect Alex's job performance though. It was most likely due to the fact that Alex looked at the manager as a father figure, so Alex did everything the manager told him to. Now, ten years later, Alex is the majority share-holder of the Central Bank's shares, which made him quite wealthy.

Alex's attitude changed as well. Gone was the boy that cared about his freedom. Now he was a man of responsibility and authority.

Alex's only regret was that he threw Lily away like a rag doll, all for the sake of his "freedom". *I wonder how Lily is doing?*

"Mr. Alex, you have a meeting scheduled with Mr. Logan for this afternoon. Will you be able to make it?"

Alex's thoughts were interrupted by Rose. Rose is the woman who first greeted Alex when he came to apply for a job at the bank. Later, when Alex became a manager, Alex decided to make Rose his secretary. She was cute with a good figure and long brown hair. Alex took notice of her professional qualities instead. She was: well-organized and put together. She could do multiple things at once, which Alex greatly appreciated. Rose was, without exaggeration, Alex's hands and feet. Meanwhile, Alex is the one doing almost all the paperwork. Of course he was completely oblivious to the fact that Rose has a huge crush on him.

"No, unfortunately I won't be able to meet Mr. Logan this afternoon. Please reschedule it for tomorrow. I want to visit my family. I haven't visited them once in ten years, and I feel extremely guilty."

"Sure, no problem."

"Thanks Rose, you're the best. I don't know what I would do without

you."

With that, Alex was out the door in a flash, not noticing the blush on

Rose's cheeks.

As Alex was driving to his hometown in his Mercedes, all his memories of the past resurfaced. He remembered the picnic date, the break-up and the exile from the village. He remembered how arrogant he was, and how terrible he treated everyone. *When I see everyone, I*

will definitely ask for forgiveness. Alex said to himself firmly deciding to do just that.

When Alex got close to the village, he parked and stepped out of his car. As he got close to the village he was hit with a wave of nostalgia. For a while Alex just stood there, taking in the fresh air.

Alex could hear the laughter and giggles of the children as they played outside. Suddenly one of the children stopped and approached Alex.

"Uncle, are you lost?" the child asked curiously.

"No I am not, but thanks for the help kiddo. Where are your parents?" "My parents? They're out in the fields working. Do you know them?" Instead of answering right away Alex asked, "What are their names?" "Arthur and Lily." the child answered innocently.

So Lily has gotten married and had a kid huh? It's not surprising it has been 10 years after all.

The child looked at Alex intensely while the other was in deep thought. Then Alex turned to the kid and asked, "Do you have any brothers and sisters?"

"Yes, I have two brothers and three sisters." At this point the child's curiosity got the better of him and he asked, "Uncle how do you know my parents?"

"I am an acquaintance of theirs, I guess you could say." Alex replied, not wanting to disclose too much information about the past. He is talking to a kid after all.

Finally, Alex turned to leave and said as a farewell, "Say hi to your mother for me"

"Alright I will. Bye uncle"

With that Alex left. The kids returned to their games. As Alex was walking to his car a single thought occupied him. *I am glad you are happy Lily. I am sorry for everything evil that I have done towards you.*

I wish I would have realized what kind of treasure trove you are sooner. However, now it is too late. The past cannot be changed. I promise myself if an opportunity presents itself, then I will not repeat the same mistake again.

With renewed determination in his eyes Alex started the drive back to the city, which was three hours away.

EPILOGUE

Sitting at the kitchen table of his house, Alex was in deep contemplation[while sipping on a cup of red wine]. *What's the point of life? I have this big house, but no wife, no kids, no grandkids. How foolish was I when I rejected Lily and the prospect of a family for the illusion of freedom? Now I have the freedom, but no one to share it with. How do I solve this issue? I can't just put a girl in a bag and bring her home saying, "Congratulations! You're my wife now!" Can I?* For a moment Alex paused, as if contemplating the consequences. *Nah, that's stupid. Besides, it will not achieve anything, only earning her wrath.* While still in thought, Rose's figure came to mind. *Maybe her? What the hell, why not. What's the worst that could happen? She rejects me? Anyway, it's like a coin toss. You win some, you lose some.* With determination Alex pulled out his phone and dialed Rose's phone number.

Alex waited patiently as the phone rang. Suddenly, the phone stopped ringing and a pleasant female voice came out the other end.

"Mr. Alex, what a pleasant surprise. Why are you calling at such a late hour? Did something happen?"

Alex waited for a bit, gathering his thoughts, and then said, "Rose I don't know how to say this, so I'll just say it like it is." There was a pause. Alex took a deep breath and continued, "Rose, will you marry me?"

There was a pause once again this time from Rose. Nobody said anything for a long time. Finally, Rose spoke, "Shouldn't we date first? After all, we barely know each other."

Alex responded, "I agree that that is the conventional way of doing things but I don't want to do it that way. Besides, if we're married couldn't we date without restrictions? I much prefer it that way. If you don't want to marry me I understand. However, with you by my side, I feel that not only will we be able to build a family, but will I gain peace and greater achievements than ever before? What do you say?"

BONUS CHAPTER I

ARTHUR- KNIGHT IN SHINING ARMOR

Disclaimer! Arthur's point of view *I never thought that I would come back here again.* As I walked through the village I reminisced about my childhood and my pre-army days. The last memory I have is my parents wishing me farewell as they saw me off.

Unfortunately, good things never last. Six months before I am discharged with honors, I get mail that informs me of my parents' demise, noting that it's most likely due to illness. Hence why I showed up here, desiring to honor their memory and visit the graveyard.

As I got to the graveyard, I noticed that right next to me stood a beautiful woman with blond hair. Seeing the sorrow on her face, I bow down slightly and express my condolences for her loss.

I don't know why, but this woman starts telling me everything all at once. I assume she was extremely lonely. From what I gathered here is what happened: Some jerk Alex dumped her, which broke her heart. After that incident it took a very long time to get over him. She must have loved Alex very much. Then when it seemed like she was ready to move on, an epidemic struck this village. The disease claimed the lives of most of the elders and some young people. Among the victims were the parents of Alex and her father.

Since my parents died from an illness as well, we were able to find common ground fairly quickly. After that, we got even closer and I asked her to marry me.

"I do!" as Lily said the magic words I leaned in for a kiss. One thing is for sure, I am the happiest man alive. I don't know what it was, but I couldn't leave my wife alone. It was as if I was pulled to her by an invisible magnet. My wife is the most beautiful woman ever. After giving birth, it was as if she was reborn with a new glow around her which attracted me even more. I truly feel blessed because Lily gave me six beautiful children[three boys and three girls]. I will protect them with my life.

BONUS CHAPTER II

A SUDDEN PROPOSAL!

Disclaimer! Rose's point of view

On this day I got off work as usual. I continued to follow my daily routine of heating my food in the microwave and watching some soap operas on tv. Then I went in to take a bath. As I got out of the shower with a towel wrapped around my waist, my phone rang on my bedside table. I picked it up, not expecting the caller to be Mr. Alex.

"Mr. Alex, why are you calling at this late hour? Did something happen?"

"Rose I don't know how to say this, so I'll just say it like it is" There was a pause on the other side of the phone. At this point my mind is racing.

Why does Alex sound so serious?

"Will you marry me?" *WHAAAAAAAAT! Marry Alex! I mean I like him and all, but marriage? WE BARELY KNOW EACH OTHER! Calm down down Rose you got this act cool.*

"Shouldn't we date each other first?"

"I agree that that is the conventional way of doing things but I don't want to do it that way. Besides, if we're married couldn't we date without restrictions? I much prefer it that way. If you don't want to marry me I understand. However, with you by my side, I feel that not only will we be able to build a family, but will I gain peace and greater achievements than ever before? What do you say?"

What should I do? What should I do? WHAT SHOULD I DO? If I don't say anything he might perceive it as a rejection. Besides, if I refuse I am doing myself a disservice. It's decided then. With determination, I spoke the words that would change my life forever.

BONUS CHAPTER III

AN ACQUAINTANCE?

Disclaimer Lily's point of view

The day started as usual. Arthur and I had some breakfast, fed our kids and told them to play outside while Arthur and I work in the fields. When we returned from the fields, our eldest son said that he had met an acquaintance of our family. He said that it was a guy with broad shoulders in a suit. Arthur and I looked at each other in confusion. Did we have an acquaintance? Our son continued by saying that the man said that he is originally from here and that he knows me.

I froze for a second, *No way! It can't be! Could it really be him?*

"Oh yea I almost forgot, the uncle said to say hi to you" My son's words brought me back to reality.

"Could it really be Alex?" Arthur chimed in.

"I am 80 percent sure that it is him."

"What do you want to do?"

"Nothing" I wrapped my arms around my husband's neck and kissed him passionately. He wasn't against it. "I am happy here with you."

"Nobody comes in for at least an hour!" said Arthur as he carried his wife to the bedroom in a princess carry. The eldest son stood there stupefied. *Oh, not this again!*

AFTERWORD

Thank you very much for reading another one of my books. Did you like it, or was it cringe? Nevertheless, thank you.

I want to let you know now that I have an animation YouTube channel(Hopefully I have at least 1,000 subs by the time this book comes out. Vaminationz is the name). Finally, I will be working on a translation of *How My Brain Works* to Russian because of all the demand. See you all in the next one.

www.ingramcontent.com/pod-product-compliance
Lightning Source LLC
LaVergne TN
LVHW021747060526
838200LV00052B/3525